Raju

The Elephant that wept

true story of Raju

Written by Angela Frank

Illustrated by Maria Florian

Angel's art club publishing

Raju

The Elephant that wept

Written by Angela Frank

Illustrated by Maria Florian

Printed in the United States of America
on paper from sustainable sources
with self-disolving eco friendly inks.
©Author Angela Frank
Illustrations Maria Florian

Adapted in to English: Filitsa Mullen-Sofianos

Book design: Fylatos
Pulishing © Angel's Art club
thessaloniki 2015

site:http://aggelikipapadopoulou.wixsite.com/angela-frank
e-mail: gelafrank@hotmail.com

twitter: https://twitter.com/gelafrank

isbn 978-960-9691-04-8
23 March 2015 Athens

RAJU
THE ELEPHANT THAT WEPT

ANGELA FRANK

Illustrations by: Maria Florian

Angel's art club publishing

Animals should live in their natural habitats and be allowed to roam freely. They don't belong in the zoo nor the circus.

Dedicated to Raju,
the elephant
who stole our hearts
when he wept
during his rescue.

Days and nights pass in agony for **Raju** the elephant.

He is the sweetest creature who roves the streets performing his act, like so many other circus animals, so that his masters can make money.

At night, chained behind a shed, next to a small tree, he travels in his imagination.

Raju dreams that he is running with his friends in the fields, that he is playing and enjoying himself surrounded by his family. He dreams of all the things that animals do when they are free in their natural environment.

But all these years his dreams remain bound as he himself is bound. And there is no help from anywhere.

Raju suffers patiently. They all pass by and he entertains them like a clown.

Only Rosie, a beautiful bird with melodious voice, talks to him when she is in India, Raju's country.

For years now, Rosie is Raju's only companion. She is his dream, his wind, his hope for freedom. Rosie is freedom.

"Animals must be free, do you hear me?" Raju tells pretty Rosie who perches on his back scratching her beak.

"I know this better than you, my darling," she says. And saying this, she circles over Raju' s head, so he can hear her song.

"Raju, I will take you away

From here, far away.

There by the river shore

Your spirit will soar

And there on the sand

I will build us a shrine

And together we'll stand

To gaze at the stars

How they sparkle and shine

On the river waters."

"You know this cannot be, my darling," he says, lowering his head until his trunk touches the ground. He doesn't want Rosie to see how sad he is.

"We must try, Raju, don't give up. Please, my sweet, don't lose hope."

"You better go, Rosie. It is night now. If my master sees you, he may catch you, too."

"I'm going, but we will meet again tomorrow. Goodnight," she twitters and disappears in the dark.

Raju finds it difficult to sleep with his feet bound by heavy chains.

He remembers the time when he was little. He remembers his mother and father, his brothers and sisters. He remembers all the beautiful and tender moments he has lived with them. For years now those images, those moments of tenderness and companionship are played over and over again in his mind.

He ponders how violently these people tore him away from the love of his family, from tenderness, dignity and the right to a free life.

They brought him to the city to exploit him.

"But why is it so?" he wonders day and night. "How can people cause so much pain? And yet there were those who caressed me and turned their faces away with tears in their eyes. But where are those kind ones? Where are they?" Raju asks.

And then he whispers: "What fate is written in the stars for me?"

As he says this, a tear rolls slowly down his cheeks.

Who says that animals can't feel? Who says that animals can't sense? Who says that animals can be abused? Who has given people the right to do that?

Next day, Rosie finds Raju in the market entertaining tourists.

"My sweet Raju, why are you gloomy? It's a beautiful day. Look at the sun! Shall I sing for you?" she asks as she warbles to ease Raju's pain.

"Oh, my Rosie, it's not only my body that hurts, it is my soul, too. And this pain in my soul is the worse of the two, the more unbearable of the two."

His feet hurt where the chains have chaffed them, but there is no one to soothe them.

His chained legs are too heavy to walk. But his spirit wants to fly, wants to escape this torture.

He read once: *"Unhappy is he who waits for someone else to give him happiness. If he doesn't take his life into his own hands, nothing will change."*

This thought turns in his head all day and all night, as Raju tries to find a solution. He believes that he must fight for his rights the same way people do. "Perhaps I should go to court or to the police?" he wonders whispering.

In the evening, Rosie brings water from the river, mixes it with soil and turns it into thick clay to smear on Raju's feet, to heal them.

"Thank you, my sweet," whispers Raju. He has no strength to speak up, no more will to live.

"Ah, no giving up!" Rosie has barely time to finish her sentence. She hides quickly in the bushes when she sees Raju's master coming to with dry leftovers for the elephant's dinner.

"Here, eat!" he growls throwing the food on the ground before him.

"Is this what you are eating? You, a king?" says Rosie as soon as the master leaves. "Just wait here!"

Before the little elephant has time to say anything, Rosie returns carrying bananas and mangos and all kinds of sweet fruit to please her dear friend.

"Oh, my dear Rosie, you are the sweetest!"

Then Rosie brings out a big envelope from under her wing. She opens it and starts reading to Raju.

"Dear Ms. Rosie Rosefinch, we have received your letter and were very upset about the condition of your friend Raju the elephant. We will send our representative to talk to Raju's master and try to talk some sense into him."

"You see?" says Rosie, smiling. "They will help you for a better life."

"I don't want a better life, Rosie. I want to be free!"

"Perhaps if we blow many helium balloons we may be able to lift you up and run away?

"Ha, ha, ha!" Raju snorted loudly.

"What if I call the other elephants, then? Something may come of it!" says Rosie excited.

"Wow, perfect! Perhaps this is the solution to my predicament," Raju agrees and his face takes on a glow, a smile of optimism, a hope.

"We must do something fast. I want to be cheerful and happy when I leave for Europe, my Raju."

"Is it time for you to go again? You know I will miss you. I always miss you when I lose you in the winter," confesses Raju.

So, Rosie, with the help of the other birds, sends messages to all the elephants.

The big day has finally come when the elephants are to rescue Raju.

But Raju's master has found out their plan and has managed to chase them away before they even set foot into town.

From that day on, Raju feels melancholy. He will not even look at the rainbow in the sky the way he used to, following it with his eyes and wondering where it comes from.

"Come my darling, you will see, next time we will have more luck. We will make it."

The day of parting has arrived. Rosie is leaving for warmer climates. But they will see each other again soon.

"Raju, I hope you will be fine until I am back," says Rosie sweetly, warbling around him.

Raju does not speak. He sits in a corner with his head low, disappointed. "It's all over," he thinks.

Rosie does not want to give him false hopes but she has a plan. If it works out she will manage to set her friend free.

"Be careful. I will be back soon," she says kissing his trunk.

"Don't worry. There is nowhere I can go. I will stay here and wait for you. Fly high, Rosie, very high and then come back and tell me how the world looks from up there . . ."

Rosie's plan is to inform the children. That's right, the children. Because only children can understand the language and the spirit of the animals.

All around the world a group is formed, a group to set Raju free, an organization for all animals held in captivity.

The children are determined to give an end to the slavery of animals. They are determined to see the animals back where they belong: in their natural habitat. Not in the circus nor at the zoo.

All of Raju's little friends across the world are getting ready. They have named their organization "Animals free."

Rosie is now certain. Raju is not alone.

In the meantime in India, Raju has taken his fate into his own hands. He decides to practice what he has read about making ourselves happy and not waiting for others to give us happiness.

One day as he is walking in the crowded market place, he manages to trick his master and escapes his attention. He approaches a policeman.

"Hello, officer! Could I have a moment, please? I would like to file a complaint."

"You? A complaint? Why?"

"Because I don't want to be tied. I want to be free!"

So, while Raju's master looks on in complete surprise, Raju gives all the information to the officer. The officer fills out the form and stares severely at Raju's master.

"Sir, I would ask you not to leave town. You may have to appear in court."

Raju's master is furious:

"You have ruined me! What do you think you are doing? I'll show you! What? Do you think you have rights? The judges will laugh at you. Unheard of! An elephant filing a complaint!"

"Let them laugh. I am not afraid anymore. Do whatever you will. I am tired of you speaking to me harshly and treating me badly. Enough!"

As he says this and for the first time in his life of captivity, Raju stands up and walks with his head held high, so high as if he is going to fly, as if he has sprouted wings.

For the first time he feels the wings of freedom carrying him high into the sky, all the way to the stars.

Time is passing in the same cheerless way as before. Raju anxiously awaits the day of the trial.

It is then that Rosie returns from her travels, bringing with her the children from the organization "Animals free."

"We are with you, Raju! You are not alone," the voices of the children ring out.

The court day is here. The calendar reads July 4th.

The lovable elephant is ready as are his many friends. His friends are all the people who help animals and fight for their rights, so that they can live free and not in captivity.

The courtroom is packed to the ceiling. It is full of people and animals from the four corners of the earth. The dolphins are waiting anxiously in the sea but they are close by, eager to show their support.

The presiding judge is Mr. Leo. Public prosecutor is Ms. Jill. The other two judges are Mr. Rabatou and Mr. Cobu.

Raju's lawyer is Ramba.

The master's defense lawyer is Mr. Ahmabat.

As the courtroom is filling with people and animals, in the square outside the courthouse others are holding big signs. The signs read

Animals belong in nature!
No more animal abuse!

Then something unexpected happens. People and animals start sitting in rows on the ground. They sit without speaking, trying to send a message by their presence.

With this silent demonstration they ask for justice, not only for Raju the elephant, but for all those other Rajus around the world.

Inside the courtroom the tension reaches its peak when Raju's lawyer asks the master:

"Will you, please, tell the court why you kept Raju in captivity for so many years?"

"Big deal," Raju's master sniggers. "It's only an animal."

Commotion and voices of protest rise in the room.

"Silence in the court or we will go to closed session," roars out Judge Leo.

The rest of the trial is conducted tensely as the master tries in vain to come up with excuses for Raju's treatment.

The character witnesses for Raju are many . . . Many? All of those present, people and animals, the police officer, the chief of police, the children from the animal rights organization speak on behalf of Raju. And Rosie narrates movingly to the smallest detail Raju's suffering as she has witnessed it all these years.

Raju waits anxiously for the verdict.

The jury retires. Inside and outside the courthouse there is great commotion.

Finally the moment of the verdict comes. The presiding judge is holding the piece of paper in his hand.

Everyone stands up in attention. The master starts to tremble. Raju waits quietly.

The judge reads the verdict slowly:

"The court, after hearing all witnesses, has decreed that Mr. Boo is guilty of the following:

1st Illegal confinement of Raju the elephant.

2nd Abuse of Raju the elephant.

3rd Exploitation of Raju the elephant.

4th Disregard for the dignity of Raju the elephant.

"As a result, the court sentences the defendant, Mr. Boo, to imprisonment and a fine of one million rupees."

Then the honorable judge turns and addresses the elephant. "Raju, you are free to live as you like," he says.

Shouts of cheers echo everywhere. Raju walks to his former master and speaks to him calmly: "So, your name is Boo?"

The chains are finally removed from Raju's feet. As the children unlock them, Raju weeps a big tear. It is a tear of joy, a tear of gratitude, the tear of freedom.

"This earth needs all of us, people and animals," says Raju. "Respect towards animals is a sign of civilization!" he trumpets for everyone to hear. And then, together with Rosie and the whole crowd that has gathered around him to welcome him into his new free life in nature, he starts to sing:

Animals can feel.

Animals can sense.

Animals shall live in harmony with people.

The

End

Angela Frank
(educator -writer)
I was born and grew up in Thessaloniki, a historic and inspirational city of North Greece.As a child I had a creative imagination and I was always making out tales to play with my younger brother, Jim. I love to dig out different, exciting heroes from my imagination and give them life on paper- writing tales, theater plays and scenarios for kid's movies. I enjoy to discover and dream new stories along with my young friends at my workshops of creative writing, 3d animation, educational programs. I strongly believe that through our civilization and art we can present and provide a better world to our kids. Through my experience of being so close with youngsters so many years , I've learn thatour children don't respond to just a plain lesson but to role models which have the power to instill and inspire the values of life needed for someone to be happy.In a few days ,my new book will be on the bookshelves. I hope you enjoy the adventure only a book can create to our imagination with me . Through my journey to youngster education so far, I've written following fairy tales which have been published and received great acceptance from my young readers.
2009 " Η παρέα της Φραντζέλας"a tale talking about three naughty little goats trying to cultivate a
biological farm.
2011 'Franzela's Friends and the biological farm" theater play for childen. it was transferred on Olympic Museum stage 2011-2012.
2011 'Santa Claus and the little ghost' : a funny Christmas related story
2014 "Ένας αστακός ιππότης και ο ιππόκαμπος ο Χιώτης"
2015 "Lonnie the Lobster Knight and a Seahorse from the Isle of Wight"
2015 "Οι νεραιδούλες της Ζωής"a fairy tale dedicated to my beloved niece.
2015 "Raju the elephant that wept"
2015 "Ρατζού ο ελέφαντας που δάκρυσε"

My name is Maria Florian and I was born and raised in Greece.I studied 3D animation at IEK Akmi (Athens) and later attended Florina School of Fine Arts (Department of Visual and Applied Arts, University of Western Macedonia), where I recently graduated from. Over the past few years I have illustrated children's books, written by myself or by other authors. My latest work is "Raju the Elephant That Wept: True Story of Raju the Elephant", by Angela Frank and ''Dreams of happiness and sadness'' by Natassa Simeonidou. "Ο καλός μας κύριος ύπνος που χάθηκε"Νίκη Δαγδαλιανίδου.

Currently I'm working on a illustration contest and installations with main theme characters from children's books.You can watch my Thesis Project , if you'd like ! All you have to do is follow my links!!
http://tsikouri.deviantart.com/

https://www.facebook.com/illustrations.of.dreams

illustrations of dreams